Rise and Shine Bunny

by Susan Talkington

illustrated by Anne Thornburgh

GT
PUBLISHING
New York

Text copyright © 1997 GT Publishing Corporation
Illustrations copyright © 1997 Anne Thornburgh.
All rights reserved.
Designed by Lara S. Demberg.
No part of this book may be used or reproduced in any manner
whatsoever without written permission from the publisher. For information, address
GT Publishing Corporation, 16 East 40th Street, New York, New York 10016.

D1416350

The dawn awoke bright and early, but Gus did not. His mother gently patted his back and said, "Gus, my love, time to get up."

"No-o-o-o," wailed Gus as he drew his blanket around himself tightly. "It's to-o-o early!"

"Now sweetie, the early bunny gets the sweet clover," his mother reminded him.

"Aw, he's just a grump, Mama..." piped up Roberta, Gus's sister, as her head popped up next to Gus's bed. Gus's brothers, Ricky and Rocky, hopped in to join the teasing and cried, "Grumpy Gus! Grumpy Gus!"

Suddenly, Gus leaped up shouting, "Go away! You are the meanest bunnies in the whole world!" His family stared at Gus in amazement as his face contorted with anger.

"G-g-golly, g-g-Gus," Ricky finally stammered, "you'd better be careful or your face will freeze that way."

"I don't care!" With that Gus turned over on his tummy, yanking the covers up so high that his little cottontail peeked out from beneath the carrot-colored comforter.

Roberta said, "Boy, someone's gonna lose his carrot cake privileges for dessert if he doesn't shape up!"

Mama sat down next to Gus and softly asked, "Gus, precious, wouldn't it be just horrible if there was no one to wake you up in the morning?"

Gus pulled the pillow off his head. "No," he snapped. "It would be wonderful! I can't think of anything nicer in the whole wide world!"

Even Roberta was speechless, but, as usual, Mama knew exactly what to say. "Well, Gus, I hope your wish never comes true. Since it's obvious you got up on the wrong side of bed this morning, I want you to take a nap so that when you wake up again, you'll choose to get up on the right side."

Gus beamed with delight. He made a production of plumping his pillows, arranging his covers just so, and snuffling down in the mattress. With a sigh, Mama shooed the other children out and quietly closed the door.

The sun hung high in the sky when Gus woke up from his nap. Gingerly lifting one corner of the covers, the little rabbit peeked out at his room. Seeing no one there, he tried to smile widely but found that his face wanted to curve down instead of up. "No matter," he declared as he bounced out of bed. "I'm by myself in my own room! This is going to be a great day!"

  As Gus hip-hopped through the burrow he shared with his family, he noticed that he was completely alone—no mama, no pesky sister, no bothersome brothers. He was so happy about this that his fluffy cottontail twitched with excitement. But not for long.

When Gus opened the front door to go outside, he glanced in the mirror and his tail almost fell off from the shock of what he saw. His face was frozen into a frown! No matter how hard he tried to smile, his mouth would only frown. The corners sagged lower and lower until Gus felt as sad as he looked. "Was Ricky right?" he wondered. "Will my face always look like this?"

Dragging himself outside, Gus saw a signpost proclaiming:
NOW ENTERING GRUMPYVILLE, HOME OF THE
GRUMPALUMPS—NO SMILING ALLOWED!

"No smiling allowed?" Gus was startled. He thought,
"I love to smile and to laugh, just not in the morning."

A nearby green expanse of clover grabbed Gus's attention. Ambling slowly into the middle of the field, he was joined by two of the unhappy Grumpalumps with their faces frozen into the same grumpy frown as Gus's. He opened his mouth wide and took a large bite of the delicious-looking plant.

"Yuck," complained Gus, barely able to swallow the mouthful. "This clover is sour!"

"What do you expect?" grumbled one of the Grumpalumps.

"Yeah, everybody knows that the early bunny gets the sweet clover," groused his friend.

Gus sniffed back a tear as he remembered his mother giving him the same advice. "Well," he said, feeling quite sorry for himself, "I suppose I'll just have to settle for a big piece of carrot cake."

Both Grumpalumps snorted and chided Gus. "There's no carrot cake here. Nobody's sweet enough to make any!"

Gus shuffled back to his home. He knew a big bunny-hug from his mother would make him feel better, but she was still no where to be found. The burrow was very lonely without the sounds of his brothers and sister. He even missed Roberta's chattering. Collapsing onto his bed, he sobbed, "Oh, if I had only listened to Mama and Roberta, or even Ricky and Rocky! I don't belong here. I'm not a Grumpalump! I'm not!"

Gus's shoulders heaved as he cried, until slowly, steadily, the tears stopped and were replaced by the gentle sound of snoring which continued for quite some time.

Gus awoke with a start. Where was he? It felt like his bed with his carrot-colored comforter. And there were his Power Rabbit action figures. But was it really his room? Determined to find out, Gus started to jump out of bed, then stopped. "I'd better make sure to get out on the right side of the bed," he announced to no one in particular.

"I'm not a Grumpalump," Gus declared as he put his left paw on the hard-packed dirt floor. "I do like to smile," he added as his right paw hit the ground. "I want to be the early bunny who eats the sweetest clover," Gus repeated leaving the bed. "And I do want to see my family again," he sniffed as he approached the doorway. "I do, I do, I do!"

Gus gulped and then, summoning all the courage he could find in his little bunny body, slowly opened the door.

There were Mama, Roberta, and even Ricky and Rocky, all sitting down to eat.

Gus looked in the mirror on the wall and stretched his face into the largest smile he could manage. "Look," he said. "I'm smiling. My face isn't frozen into a frown! It was, but not anymore."

"Oh, Mama," Gus cried as he gave his mother a huge hug,
"it was horrible to wake up without all of you around!"
"But, dear, we're all here . . ." his mother began.

"And Roberta, did you know that there is a place where no one is sweet enough to make carrot cake and the only clover is sour and no one is allowed to smile?"

Gus stopped to catch his breath and realized that his family was staring at him as if he were making no sense.

Roberta looked up from her dinner and stared curiously at her brother. "Gus, you had better sit down and have something to eat and explain what you're babbling about. Mama, don't you think he needs to have an extra large piece of carrot cake?"

Grumpy Gus was never seen again and Grateful Gus, who always ate the sweetest clover with the largest smile imaginable, stayed forever.